For our daughter Marley.

Explorers are we, intrepid and bold,
Out in the wild, amongst wonders untold.
Equipped with our wits, a map and a snack,
We're searching for fun and we're on the right track!

- Bill Watterson

JASPER'S GREAT CANADIAN ADVENTURE

Book 1: Jasper Explores the Rocky Mountains

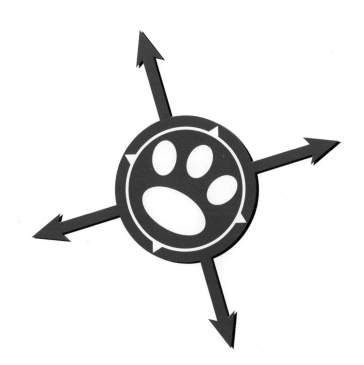

by Doug and Shannon Chapman,
Explorers Are We Inc.

This is the story of a very small bear
and how he came to find his way in a great big world.

This bear we speak of?   His name is Jasper.
Well, at least he's pretty sure that's what his name is.

Jasper had heard people say that word a lot
and they must have been talking about him.

"After all," he thought to himself,
"I am the only one sitting here."

You see Jasper was visiting the National Parks in the Canadian Rocky Mountains with his Little Girl and her family. Jasper loved playing outside in the fresh mountain air. Very much so!

Jasper loved hugging Little Girl and she loved hugging Jasper.
The two loved each other very much.

"Where did Little Girl go?" Jasper asked. He had heard Dad say something about ice cream. "Yum! Make mine Bear's Claw please," Jasper said. "It's my favourite."

Jasper waited on the bench for his tasty treat.
He thought they would be right back, but Mom and Dad didn't come right back.
Not with Bear's Claw ice cream and most importantly, not with Little Girl.

Jasper climbed down from the bench.

He walked up to a friendly-looking elk to ask him for help.
"Excuse me sir, have you seen Little Girl?" Jasper asked.

"_____", the elk just stared blankly and sniffed the Lost Polar Bear.

The friendly-looking elk was friendly indeed. He didn't mean to be rude;
it's just that he didn't speak Cuddle Buddy and Jasper? Well, he couldn't speak Critter.

"Uhh?... Okay then? Well thanks anyway Mr. Elk!" Jasper shrugged.

"I suppose I'll have to find
Little Girl on my own."

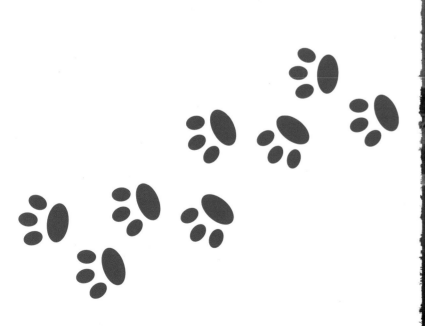

"Maybe they got on a bus?" Jasper wondered.
"But which bus could it be? All the buses look the same to me!"

Jasper looked under a rock. He looked behind a tree.
Frustrated, the small bear cried, "Where could Little Girl be?!"

Jasper sat quietly on the rocky shore by Spirit Island.

He wondered if he'd ever see Little Girl again,
but as he did, the rolling waves of Maligne Lake
reminded him of the Big Water near Home.

"THAT'S IT!" Jasper cheered,
"If I can find Big Water, then Little Girl will find me!"

Jasper wasn't too sure where Big Water was, so he pulled out a map from his Handy Backpack. It was a Handy Backpack indeed, as it carried everything a small bear could ever need for a Great Adventure.

Of course being a bear, Jasper couldn't read that well, but he knew that the colour blue on his map meant water.

"There sure are a lot of blue spots on my map," Jasper said.

"I guess I'll have to check them one by one."

And so off he went to do just that.

Jasper followed the highway along until he came to a lake hidden deep in the mountains.

He climbed up a rocky staircase and watched as happy families canoed on Moraine Lake below.

Was this Big Water?

Jasper found a canoe of his own to see for himself.

With paddle in paw, Jasper paddled across the clear, blue-green water searching for Little Girl.

"LITTLE GIRL, WHERE ARE YOU?!" echoed across the quiet lake as the Lost Polar Bear called in vain.

Jasper left his canoe behind to search
for higher ground.

He climbed and he climbed until he found
a sign post at the top of the world.
From way up there, Jasper saw
another beautiful lake.

"Could that be Big Water?"
the small bear wondered.
"I suppose there's only one way to find out."

And so off he went to check it out.

Jasper ventured on to Lake Louise.
The icy, blue lake was formed
from a giant ice cube called a glacier.
As the glacier melted the water ran
down the mountain and pooled below.

Was this Big Water?

Jasper decided to stick
a paw in to test the water.

"Brrr!... too COLD!" he shivered.

Jasper checked his map again and pushed further on down the road.

"My fur's looking kind of dirty," Jasper thought to himself.
"After all, I have been hiking and climbing all day." He was about due for Tubby Time.

The crashing waterfall at Johnston Canyon was too rough for a bath,
so Jasper continued on his trek until he reached Banff, Canada's highest town.

"Phew! What's that smell?" Jasper said as he scrunched up his nose.
"It's not me, so what could it be?" It was the sulfur from the hot springs.
You see Banff is famous for its natural hot pools. The bubbling, warm water flows
from underground streams, but it can be kind of stinky.

Was this Big Water?

Jasper climbed in to see for
himself... and to get scrubby
of course.

"Whew!... too HOT!"
he sighed.

Jasper was tired from his long journey, so he decided to find a place to make camp.

"It's not Big Water, but it'll make a nice home for tonight," the Lost Polar Bear yawned, as he placed his Handy Backpack on the prickly pine needle floor.

Jasper was trying to be brave, but he was so lonely.
He knew that somewhere Little Girl was looking for him.
She would be sad and that made him feel very sad indeed.

Jasper missed hugging Little Girl and she missed hugging Jasper.
The two missed each other very much.

Jasper was chopping wood for a campfire when suddenly he heard a scary sound.

SNAP!

"What was that?" Jasper said as his ears rose alertly.

CREEEEK!

"There it is again!" he exclaimed.

POP!

"Yikes!!"

Jasper could feel that someone or some Thing was watching him.

The Polar Bear trembled as he whispered, "It's a... MONSTER?!"

"No monster's going to make a meal out of me,"
Jasper told himself. "I'll set a trap for him!"

Jasper took a rope from his Handy Backpack and got to work.
It was times like this that Jasper was glad he was an expert knot-tier.
"You never know when you're going to bump into a Monster in the woods."
And with that said he quickly tied his rope and covered it with leaves.

Jasper baited his trap with Hot Chocolate.
"After all," he thought, "who can resist Hot Chocolate?"
Jasper added extra marshmallows just in case the Monster liked his that way.

"A-Ha!" Jasper cheered as the Monster took the bait. With the sound of rustling leaves, the Monster was whisked into the air.

"Hello," the upside-down Monster said. "I'm Tundra, what's your name?"

Jasper decided that Tundra wasn't a Monster at all; he was a Timber Wolf and a friendly one at that.

The pair had a lot in common. You see, Tundra was on a camping trip with his Little Boy when he lost his way. He tried to find him, but... that was a long, long time ago.

Jasper and Tundra had other things in common besides being lost. They both liked campfires and hockey ... and they both loved Hot Chocolate.

"Extra marshmallows please," Tundra said.

"I once scored 52 goals!" Tundra exclaimed. "Well I had 10 shutouts!" Jasper replied.

While the Polar Bear and the Timber Wolf bragged about game-winning goals and overtime saves, they finished their Hot Chocolate and rolled out their sleeping bags.

It was getting late and the mountains do tend to get chilly at night,
so Jasper threw another log on the campfire to keep cozy and warm.
Well, that and to keep any other would-be Monsters away.

Together the new-found friends laughed and told scary stories until dark.
Under the pale light of the northern stars, Jasper and Tundra drifted off fast asleep.

As the sun rose, Jasper and Tundra
woke to the sound of chirping birds.

After a tasty campfire breakfast of
bacon and eggs, they struck camp.

They hiked and they climbed until
the pair found themselves
at the edge of a cliff.

Through the early morning mist
they looked out over the valley below.
The forest seemed to go on forever.

"It's a great big world out there,"
the Lost Polar Bear sighed, feeling very small indeed.
"How will I ever find my way?"

"Don't worry Jasper," Tundra replied. "We'll find Little Girl together."

Jasper thought for a moment.
After a long pause, he smiled and cheered,
"Then we'd better get going!"

And with that in mind,
Jasper and Tundra set out on their Great Canadian Adventure.

Produced by Explorers Are We Inc.

National Library of Canada Cataloguing in Publication
Chapman, Doug, 1969-
Jasper explores the Rocky Mountains/by Doug and Shannon Chapman
(Jasper's great Canadian adventure: bk. 1)
ISBN 0-9733908-0-8
I. Chapman, Shannon, 1972-   II. Title.   III. Series: Chapman, Doug, 1969- Jasper's great Canadian adventure; bk.1.
PS8555.H398145J38 2004   jC813'.6   C2004-900055-1

"Jasper's Great Canadian Adventure" was created using: Nikon Coolpix 5000, Adobe Photoshop 7.0, Adobe Illustrator 10 and QuarkXPress 5.0.
Printed and bound in China by ITS Design & Printing for Explorers Are We Inc.

Explorers Are We Inc. would like to thank Dennis Johnson and Erin Woodward (Red Deer Press), Clifford L. Spyker and Patricia Robertson (MKS Learning Centre) and Allan and Diana Scott. Without their contributions, Jasper would still be sitting on the bench.

We would also like to thank Stu and Thelma Chapman (contacts and support); Geoff Coombs, Kim Pyper-Coombs and Lis Dam Lo (editors); Ron Hearnden, Kathy Lowinger, Sandi and Ron Richard, and Dale Richardson (direction); Randy Connolly and Mark Riley (instructors); and Keith Dunn (for starting an incredible chain of events).

Special thanks to The Black Crowes, Ben Harper, Jack Johnson, Lenny Kravitz, Bob Marley, Sam Roberts, Chris Robinson, Jimmy Buffett, Genesis, Brian May, Queen, Billy Idol and Steve Stevens (musical accompaniment); and to Julie Aigner-Clark, Walt Disney, Benjamin Hoff, J.K. Rowling, Bill Watterson, Nickelback, Shania Twain, Lyle Alzado, Al Davis and the Oakland Raiders (inspiration).

No stuffed animals were harmed during the making of this book
… but Doug fell down a few times.